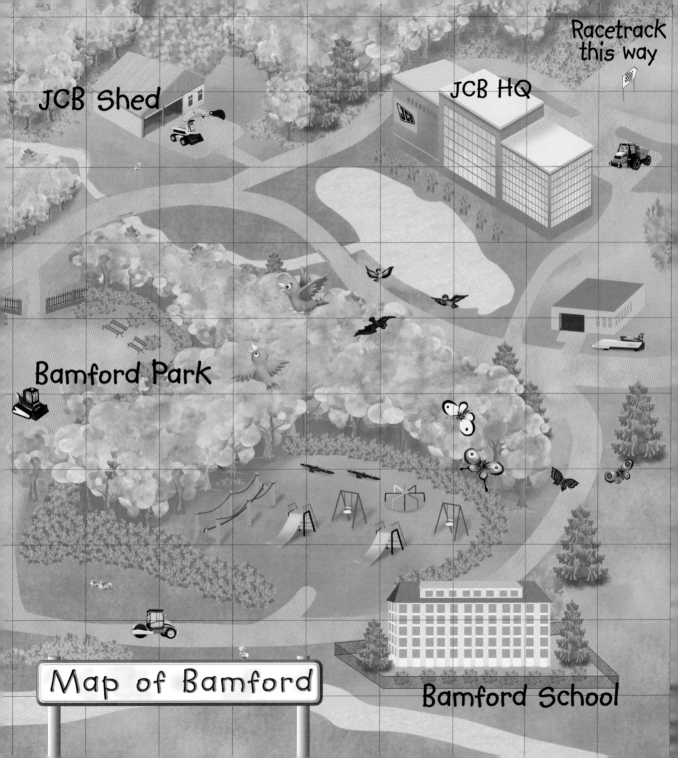

JCB Shed

Racetrack
this way

JCB HQ

Bamford Park

Map of Bamford

Bamford School

THIS BOOK
BELONGS TO

CONTENTS

GETTING IT RIGHT

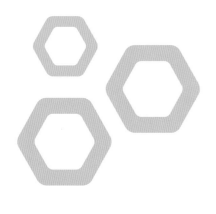

Joey was the first JCB to wake up. He wanted everyone else to be awake, too.

"Vroom, vroom! Wake up everybody!"

He vroomed again loudly. "Come on, you guys! We're doing some BIG building work today!" Joey revved. "Are you ready for that, big fella?" he asked Elvis, who was still yawning.

"You can always count on me," he chugged sleepily.

Sam arrived to lead the gang to the building site. They were working on a new road outside Bamford and needed to start work on a roundabout and a bridge. It was very exciting.

As always, Freddie and Joey zoomed ahead. Doug trundled quickly behind to keep an eye on them. Even Rex was steaming along today. He had more work to do than normal.

Roxy, Larry and Elvis arrived at the building site. Larry soon found a huge pile of pallets that needed moving. They had hundreds of pipes on them, to go under the road.

Sam called to Elvis. "Can you start by the bridge, please?" He pointed to a big area that needed digging.

Then he shouted to Roxy. She was going to be working with Joey. They had a lot to do.

As the day grew hotter and hotter, Doug took a little drive around the site to check that everyone was okay.

"How's it going?" he asked Joey and Roxy.

Roxy and Joey were shovelling and scooping as fast as they could. They had to dig ten trenches all around the site.

"We just need you now," they said
to Doug. "The trenches are finished but
we have to move all the soil out of the way."

"I'll be back to help as fast as I can,"
promised Doug.

Doug drove out to the very edge of the site where
Freddie was cutting the grass.

The grass was so long that Doug couldn't see over the top!

"Freddie, are you there?" Doug shouted. He thought he could hear
snoring.

"Hah-foo . . . hah-fffoooo . . . hah – oh – erm – yes, I'm here!"
sputtered Freddie.

Doug smiled. Freddie was a fast worker, but sometimes tried so
hard that he tired himself out.

Freddie started his blades spinning and cut his way out of
the long grass. "Nearly finished!" he said, looking a
little bit embarrassed.

"Well done, young man," said Doug. "I think
you're pulling that trailer full of kerb stones
next." He winked at Freddie and drove off
smiling.

Doug pulled up alongside Rex. "Hey, Rex, nice rolling!"

Rex put his brakes on and puffed steam from his exhaust pipe. "I'm nearly all rolled out!" he exclaimed.

"Don't you worry," said Doug. "Sam has already said what a great job you're doing. You've finished in half the time he expected!"

Rex smiled and did a little cha-cha-cha. "Then we'll be home in time for some dancing!" he said hopefully.

Larry drove past and joined in the dance. "Just a few more pipes, and I'm done!" he called happily.

"Hey, Elvis, how's it going?" shouted Doug.

Elvis just nodded and turned away to scoop up a pile of stones. "Fine," he said.

Doug, Rex and Larry looked at each other. Something was wrong. Elvis wasn't usually so quiet.

"I'll check him out," said Doug. "You guys carry on."

Doug trundled over to where Elvis was working.

"Hey big guy!" said Doug. "What's up?"

Elvis let his bucket droop. He started to speak, and then Freddie zoomed up.

"Cheer up, Elvis. You look like you've just buried your own keys!"

"Hmm," sighed Elvis. "I might as well have."

Doug and Freddie looked worried. Elvis trundled backwards and spoke quietly. "I don't know what's wrong with me," he explained. "I'm just so slow compared to you guys."

Just then, Sam ran over to speak to them.

"Freddie!" Sam called in a cross voice. "Have you still got those kerb stones?"

"No, I moved those ages ago!" said Freddie, proudly. "I put them over there."

Sam turned to look. "Well, that's why I couldn't find them," he shouted. "I asked you to put them over THERE."

Freddie looked shocked. He thought he'd been doing a really great job.

"Sorry, boss," he said sadly.

"Well, just concentrate," snapped Sam. "Next time I ask you to do something, do it properly instead of quickly."

Sam wiped his dirty hands on his trousers. "Now then," he said. "Elvis, my man. How's it going?"

Elvis revved his engine sadly. "I'm not finished yet, boss," he said.

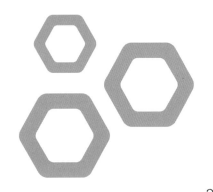

Sam smiled. He wasn't cross
any more. "I'm not surprised
you're not finished," he said. "You're
working here for a whole week. Your
work is going to take a lot longer than the
others."

Elvis cheered up. "So I'm not being slow?"

Sam patted Elvis on his huge, muddy tyre. He promised
Elvis that he wasn't being slow at all.

As Sam walked away, Doug smiled at Elvis and Freddie. Elvis
smiled back. "You can always rely on me!" he said. "After all,
what do I always say? If you're going to do a
job, let's –"

"– do the job right!" joined in
Doug and Freddie.

"And I DEFINITELY need
to remember that!" smiled
Freddie, as he zoomed off
to put the kerb stones in
their proper place.

That night, the JCB gang were glad to be back at home. They had all worked very, very hard and were hot and tired.

Cyril, the mechanic, hosed them down before bedtime. "Every single one of you needs a shower tonight!" he teased, as he sprayed them all. He tidied away his things and closed the door as he said goodnight.

When he had gone, Roxy drove into the middle of the shed. "Fancy a dance, anyone?"

"Ooh, yes!" Elvis cried, and started up his engine quietly. "Are you joining in, Freddie?" he asked, looking at the tractor watching from the edge.

"I guess," said Freddie. "As long as it's not a quickstep . . . I'd probably get it all wrong!"

FEELING GREEN

Sam pushed open the big doors of the JCB shed. It was early in the morning, and he thought they would all still be asleep.

"Morning, Sam!" chirped Joey. "Is it green day today?"

"Pardon?" asked Sam, surprised.

"Green day? Cyril said that one day this week, I'll be doing an important job with some conservation people. That's green stuff, to save the planet, isn't it?"

"Oh, yes!" agreed Sam. "You're working down by the river."

The others all crowded around Sam, wanting to know if they

were working at the river as well. They were all sad to hear that only Joey was needed there. The rest of the gang were working on the building site by the new Bamford road.

"I've never been down by the river," said Rex. "I'm always afraid I might roll in."

"Oh, it's beautiful down there," revved Joey. "It's full of trees and fish and . . . erm . . . water and things."

"Have you ever been before?" asked Elvis.

"Erm, well not actually BY the river," admitted Joey. "I've done some work in the car park though."

Roxy laughed. "It is nice down by the river, but only certain parts of it. Some bits are full of weeds and rubbish."

Joey did a little dance. "Well, I can't wait!" he said. "It's better than working on a building site every day!"

RIVER

20

Doug raised his eyebrows. Then he gathered the
gang together so they could drive to the site.

   "Bye, Joey!" they all called as they trundled off.
"Have fun!"

   "I will!" he smiled, and headed off to find Sam again.

   Sam took Joey to the river. Joey got very excited as they passed
the car park.

   It was tricky getting down to the river itself. The banks were steep
and grassy.

   "Can Freddie come to cut the grass?" asked Joey. He'd like it if he
had a friend there with him.

   Sam explained that the people in charge wanted to keep the
grass long. "It gives a home to more creatures," he said.

   Sam and Joey drove away from the steepest bit. They found a
path that led down to the edge of the water.

   "Oogh," said Joey. It smelt bad. He tried to reverse away.

"Don't drive off, Joey!" smiled Sam. "That's what you're here for. The river smells here because it is blocked up. We need you to clear it."

Joey looked at the river. It was covered in green slime. He usually loved to get dirty, but this didn't look so nice.

"Do I have to go in?" he asked.

Sam shook his head. "Just use your scoop to get rid of the soggy stuff at the edge."

Joey slowly drove to the edge and lowered his scoop. He shivered as it touched the water. It wasn't cold, but it was slimy. Yuck.

Joey spun around and Sam showed him where to tip out his load. As he let the slimy stuff fall, some brown gooey strands stuck to the edge of his scoop. He could see a snail clinging on to them. He shivered again.

Two of the conservation workers, Chris and Bob, were checking the slime. They didn't want any creatures, like the snail, to be left out of the water.

The conservationists were really pleased with Joey's work.

"You're such a good helper!" they praised. They thought it was great fun, working with a big digger like him.

Joey wasn't so sure. He hadn't moved all day. All he'd done was scoop the slime, spin around and tip it out. It might have been okay if his friends were there.

Joey wondered what Freddie, Roxy and Larry were doing. He wished he could be working hard trying to keep up with Elvis. He missed Rex's rolling songs. He even felt sorry that he didn't have Doug to boss him around.

Sam came back to check on Joey. "Good work!" he said. "Now I need to move you on to your next job."

Phew, thought Joey. No more boring scooping. They drove back to the river path and moved farther along.

The path led down to the river and
Joey parked in a safe spot on the
riverbank.

"What now?" he asked Sam. At
least he couldn't see any gooey stuff
here.

"I need you to move those plants
from the bank into the water," said
Sam. "Chris and Bob will plant them."

Joey looked at the plants. They
weren't brown and slimy – but they were green and slimy. He gave a
big sigh and picked up the first ones. He spun around and placed
them in the water.

Chris and Bob were wearing enormous wellies that reached to
their chests. They stood in the water and planted everything that
Joey gave them.

Joey felt like he had been moving wet, slimy plants and
weeds for ever. He didn't think the river was very
beautiful here, and he didn't think conservation work
was very exciting. He just missed his friends.

Finally, Joey had moved all of the plants into the river. Chris and Bob said thank you very much for being so helpful. Joey tried to smile, but he was feeling very glum.

As Sam and Joey drove back to the car park, Sam showed Joey some of the other bits of the river. "Look, that bit is beautiful!" he said, pointing to a place where the river flowed under a bridge. Joey could see silver flashes in the water.

"Fish!" he cried.

"Yes," said Sam. "And dragonflies, and butterflies, and lots of kinds of wild flowers."

Joey agreed that the river did look nice there. Perhaps he could bring his friends to this part. Sam explained that all the good work Joey had done today would help to make more of the river beautiful. Joey felt quite proud when he heard that.

They drove back to JCB HQ to find the others.

"Hey, Joey! How was the river?" asked Larry in the shed.

"Hmm . . ." said Joey. "Honestly? It was smelly and slimy. And quite boring. And I wish you lot had been there."

Larry and Roxy looked at each other.

"Anyway, how was your day?" asked Joey.

Larry and Roxy both smiled. They had been working on the drainage system next to the new road.

"Smelly and slimy!" they laughed. "But not that boring. We all got to work together all day. But we wish you had been there!"

They all laughed together. Roxy zoomed around Joey in a neat circle. "Shall we dance?" she asked.

"I'd love to," said Joey. "River Dance, anyone?!"

TYRED OUT

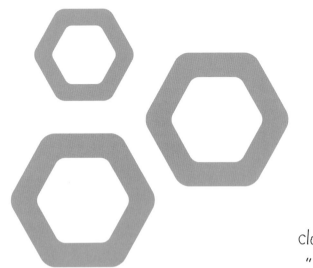

It was very early in the morning and the JCB gang were still asleep. Only Doug Dumptruck was awake.

"Hem hem vroooooom!" spluttered Doug. "Time to wake up, everybody!"

Joey opened one eye and then closed it again quickly.

"I saw that!" honked Doug. "I know you're awake, young digger! Come on, everyone. Get up!"

One by one, they all started their engines and drove out of the shed. Sam, the foreman, was walking across the yard.

"Well, you're all up early!" said Sam. "Good job, too. We have to head into town today. We're building a new car park."

"Watch out, I'm coming through!" said Doug as they all drove through the streets of Bamford. "It's a good thing I woke you all up early. We won't get stuck in the morning traffic."

Rex wasn't very fast at any time, but he felt even slower in the mornings. He trundled along near the back of the line. Freddie was behind him.

"Hurry up, Rex!" he beeped. "I'm Freddie Fastrac, and this car park needs me!"

Freddie was looking forward to working with the team. He loved it when they were all on site together.

"Right, you lot! I'm in charge here!" announced Doug, taking over.

"Roxy, I want you digging over there. Elvis, you have to dig at that side. Scoop all your dirt into me so I can move it out of the way."

Roxy zoomed over to where Doug was pointing. Elvis couldn't wait to start digging.

"Let's scoop it and move it!" he smiled.

Doug carried on giving orders. "Rex, you go there and flatten that bit. Joey, I need you to load up Freddie's trailer with dirt so he can move it out of the way. Is everybody ready?"

Joey and Freddie drove off to the other side of the building site. They both thought Doug was being a bit TOO bossy today.

As the sun rose in the sky, the piles of dirt grew bigger and bigger. The site was looking much flatter. It was going to be a very good car park for the people of Bamford.

Doug stopped working and looked around. "Larry, it's time for you to help. We need those railings moving from that pile. Put them all around the edge of the site."

"No job is too big!" Larry cried, and started lifting.

Rex was looking a bit tired.

"Wake up, Rex!" whispered Roxy. "You've nearly finished rolling already. You're doing a great job!"

"Come on, Rex!" boomed Doug's voice. "Don't slow down, there's lots to do!"

Joey was still scooping up dirt and loading it into Freddie. Freddie winked at Joey and pointed to a huge pile of soil.

Joey wondered what Freddie wanted. He followed him behind the pile and whispered, "What?"

"I'm fed up of Doug bossing us around," said Freddie. "It's making me quite cross."

"Well, he is normally quite bossy," whispered Joey. "That's just Doug."

Freddie wasn't happy. Doug was very good at his work, but today he was giving too many instructions. Freddie wanted to be left alone to do his job.

"Come on, you boys!" honked Doug. "And don't forget the safety rules when we're on site!"

Freddie let out steam from his exhaust pipe. "Pffffft!"

Freddie had an idea to teach Doug a lesson. He whispered to Joey and told him not to tell anyone else. He didn't want to get the others into trouble.

Joey grinned. It was very naughty, but maybe it would teach Doug a lesson.

Everyone was getting very hot. Cyril, the mechanic, was on site to check that they weren't getting overheated.

Doug was looking hotter than anyone else. His cabin was all misted up, and there was steam coming from under his bonnet.

"Are you alright, Doug?" asked Cyril. "You look exhausted."

Doug stopped working. "I am very tired. I don't understand it. I'm dumping as fast as I can, but that pile isn't getting any higher. And the pile over there by Elvis isn't getting smaller, even though I'm trying to move it all away."

"Well, Elvis IS the biggest digger in the team," said Cyril. "It's very hard work to move all the dirt he digs."

Just then, Freddie appeared from behind the pile of rubble that Doug was making.

"Stop right there, young Freddie!" said Cyril. "What's going on?"

"Erm, nothing ..." said Freddie.

"So why are you bringing dirt away from there? You should be helping to make that pile bigger."

Freddie lowered his eyes in shame. He looked at Joey, who had been loading up Freddie's trailer with dirt from Doug's pile.

"We ... erm ... we thought it would be funny," said Freddie.

"We thought Doug was being too bossy," said Joey.

Doug was very upset. He didn't think their trick was funny at all.

"Right," said Cyril. "I'll be in charge from now on. Freddie and Joey, I want you to move back all the dirt that you've taken away. Everybody else, it's time to go home."

It was nearly dark when Freddie and Joey finished their work. They were more tired than they had ever been. They were sorry, too, for what they'd done. They knew that they should have asked Doug not to be bossy, instead of playing a trick on him.

As they drove into the yard, they could hear disco music.

They freewheeled quietly through the big shed doors. Doug was dancing with Roxy, and looked quite happy. Larry saw them and parked next to them.

"Doug cheered up quickly when we let him choose the music," he explained. "And he's said sorry for being so bossy. He's not cross with you any more."

Just then, Doug caught sight of Freddie and Joey.

"Hey, boys! Come and dance!" he shouted to them. Then he stopped dancing for a second. "That is – if you want to. It's not an order!"

48

The Right Moves

Sam, the foreman, was in the JCB shed. He was telling everyone what they were going to be doing that day.

"Hurray! We're going to the playground!" shouted Joey.

"We're not just going to it – we're building it!" laughed Roxy. "That's my kind of work!"

The children of Bamford were getting a new play area.

The whole JCB team were going to the park, and everyone had a job to do.

"Off we go," sputtered Doug. "And remember, this playground building is serious business. Safety is the most important thing today."

It had been raining all
week and the ground
was really muddy.

"It's only mud – it
washes off!" smiled Roxy.

Joey was very happy. He
really loved working in the mud.

"Hey, Elvis – don't get stuck!"
called Joey. Elvis grinned and started
digging.

Doug had lots of earth to move, and was
working hard. Larry was busy, too, carrying wooden
poles. They were going to build swings, a
slide, and a huge climbing frame with
ropes and bridges.

Freddie was moving earth and
rocks to the edge of the site.

"Let me do that!" offered
Roxy.

"I'm fine," peeped Freddie.
"Maybe you can help Joey?"

Joey was digging a trench
around the edge of the playground.

"I'll help!" said Roxy.

"Uh-uh," said Joey, and shook his
head. Mud flew everywhere.

"I was born to dig holes. Ask Doug what to do."

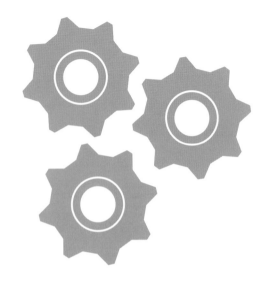

Roxy raced over to Doug. "Shall I dig
here?" she asked.

Doug honked. "No, not
there! That's where Elvis
is digging. You go and
help Larry."

Roxy trundled over to Larry. He was making neat piles of wooden poles, ready to build the climbing frame.

"Hey, Roxy!" he smiled. "Today is great fun! Are you helping Rex?"

"No," frowned Roxy. "He doesn't need me either. Can't I help you?"

"No need," said Larry. "Sam told me to pile these here and then go back to the yard to get some more. I'm all done now."

Roxy looked around for Sam. He hadn't given her a job to do. Everyone else was getting on with their work and didn't need her help.

She tried Elvis. He was her friend. Maybe he'd give her a job.

"Sorry, Roxy," puffed Elvis. "This is a BIG job. It needs the biggest digger on the team – that's me!"

Gradually, the building site started to look more like a playground. The ground was level, and the biggest poles were in place.

"Hey, big guy!" Joey shouted to Elvis. "Have you finished?"

"All done!" said Elvis. "You can always count on me!"

"What a team!" smiled Freddie. "Trust the boys to get things right! Beep! Watch out, Elvis – you nearly knocked over that swing!"

Sam arrived to see how they were doing. "Wow, fellas! You've worked well today!"

Roxy reversed out of sight. She felt so left out. It wasn't fair – she was as good as any of them.

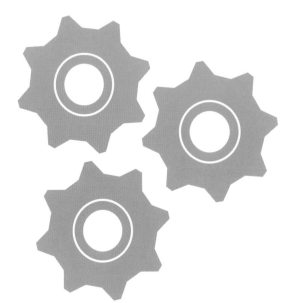

Then Roxy heard her name. Sam was calling for her.

"Here I am," she said quietly, and trundled forward.

"Right, Roxy, it's your turn now," said Sam. "These chaps are way too heavy to finish this job. They'll make a mess of our special play area."

Roxy cheered up. She listened carefully to Sam's instructions.

"I need somebody small and nimble to put the final pieces in place. Can you do it?"

"Beep, beep! I certainly can. I've got all the best moves!" Roxy couldn't wait to get started.

Roxy worked hard. She zipped around the play area, carrying pieces for the swings and slide.

She carefully dug small amounts of earth to hold all of the posts in place.

She danced around the climbing frame, making sure it was built properly for the children.

She zoomed all over the playground, scattering wood chippings on the floor. There wasn't a single bit of ground she didn't cover, nipping in and out of the posts and making sure the whole play area was soft enough. She didn't want any children to hurt themselves.

"Hey, Roxy, do you need my help?" shouted Joey.

"Thanks, Joey – but I'm fine. You'd better stay out there, like Sam said. I don't want your big tyres churning up my good work!"

When the final swing was fastened in place, Roxy drove over to her friends.

"Nice work, Roxy!" said Larry. "Just look at that for a playground!"

Roxy led the team back to the yard. As they drove through the gates, Doug beeped at her. "Just a minute, young lady!" he said.

Roxy turned around. "What?" she asked, and then peeped in surprise. Larry had picked her up and lifted her above everybody.

"Well, you might be the smallest, but you're still the best!" he smiled. The others all tooted their horns.

"Shall we dance, madam?" asked Larry.

"I'd love to," Roxy smiled. "But let's do a group dance, so that no one feels left out!"

BACK TOGETHER

As the sun rose in the sky and the birds of Bamford started to sing, the JCB gang woke up. They already knew their jobs for today. Phil, the farmer, wanted a new fence around his field.

Freddie was very excited. He was going to be working with nearly all of his friends. That was his favourite kind of work.

Rex didn't look very happy.

"What's wrong, Rex?" asked Larry.

"There isn't any work for me on the farm. I'm on my own today, working on a new road," said Rex.

"Don't worry, Rex," said Larry. "We'll see you tonight in the shed. I'm sure you'll have lots to tell us about your day."

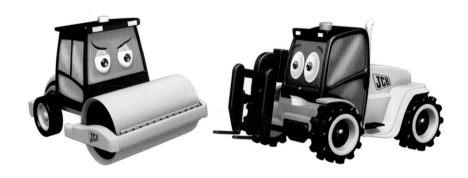

Phil, the farmer, arrived to show the gang where to go. He patted Rex on the cabin.

"Hey, big guy! Working on the roads today, aren't you? See you back here tonight, and good luck!"

Rex slowly rolled off with Sam, the foreman. The others waved goodbye.

Freddie led the way to Phil the farmer's field. Joey already had his drill fitted and was whizzing it around and around.

"Zzzzzzz! Time to drill some holes!" he cried, whizzing the drill some more.

It was a cloudy day but the gang were hot from working so hard. Joey had drilled lots of holes around the edge of the field. Now it was Roxy and Freddie's turn.

Roxy carried the fence posts. Freddie picked each one up and carefully dropped it in a hole.

Doug was in charge, as always.

"Good work, Freddie! That's right, move it slowly. Those posts need to be nice and straight!"

Larry watched the fence being built. He was fully
loaded with wire which would be fixed between the posts.

Elvis was moving large stones out of the way. The field was home
to a flock of sheep, so it needed to be safe.

The sheep were penned in next to the field. They huddled together,
wondering what was happening.

"Baa! Baa!" they cried.

Larry and Elvis moved a bit further away. Those sheep were so
noisy!

"Baa! Baa! Come baaaaack!" the sheep bleated.

Rex had nearly finished his
work. He sang a little song to
himself. He was missing his
friends, but it wasn't too bad
working alone. He rolled
backwards and forwards, humming his favourite
flattening tunes.

"Rex! Rex!" he heard Sam shouting. "We're all finished here!
Good work – well done."

Rex gave a little shudder. Rolling made him *sleepy* sometimes!

"You drive home now, and I'll be with you soon," said Sam.
"Thanks for all your hard work."

The fence was finished. It was time to move the sheep back into their field. Phil, the farmer, opened the gate.

"Baa! Baa!" the sheep cried, and all ran off together in the wrong direction. Doug blocked their way and they all turned around.

The sheep ran towards their field and through the new gate.

"Baaack! We're baaaack!" they bleated.

Then Larry noticed that one sheep had run away from the field.

"Doug! Roxy! Quick!" he beeped. He lowered his forks and chased after the sheep.

The sheep saw Larry and ran away. Larry did a quick U-turn and shouted.

"Come baaack! Oh – why am I talking like a sheep?" he peeped. "Roxy, help! It's running away!"

Rex trundled back towards the shed. He wondered how they were doing with that fence. Perhaps he could go to the farm to say, "Hello!"

As Rex got closer to the fields, he sang another song. "Rolling, rolling, rolling, I have finished rolling, I am good at rolling, I am!"

Then he heard a strange noise.

"Baa!"

Rex stopped singing.

"Baaaaaaaa!" Rex stopped rolling and listened carefully.

"Take me baaaaaaack!"

Rex rolled slowly around the corner, wondering what he would find. Then he saw a sheep in the middle of the road.

"Baaaaack! I want to go baaaaaaaack!"

Rex slowly and quietly trundled up to the sheep. It ran away.

Rex rolled after it. The sheep ran again.

Rex didn't want to hurt the sheep. Every time he got close, it ran away. It was moving in the direction of the farm, so Rex wasn't worried. He quietly herded it along, stopping and starting, as the sheep ran in front.

As Rex and the sheep got close to the field, he could hear lots of other sheep.

"Baaaack! Bring her baaaaaaack!" they were bleating.

Rex trundled forwards one more time. The sheep ran in front, and then it saw its friends. It rushed into the field and Phil, the farmer, closed the gate.

"Rex, well done! You saved the day!" cheered Roxy.

"Hurray for Rex!" shouted Larry. "It's good to have you baaaaaaack – oh, stoppit!"

TIDY UP, TIDY UP!

It was a beautiful sunny day on the farm. All the gang were working together. They were tidying up for Phil, the farmer.

Rex was rolling in the farmyard to make it nice and flat.

"Hey, Rex, look at me!" called Elvis. "I can dig and scoop at the same time! Let's scoop it and move it, double time!"

Rex smiled and carried on rolling slowly. He sang his favourite flattening songs and listened to the others shouting in the fields.

"Roxy! Hello-o-o-o!" shouted Joey. He and Larry were working together today. They were best friends. Larry was carrying lots of bales of straw.

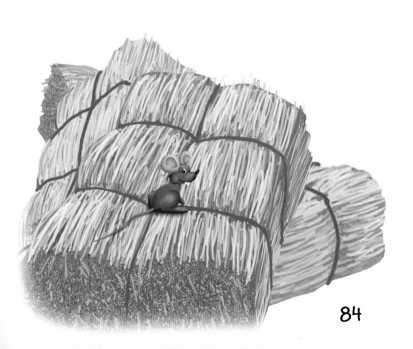

Roxy looked over. Larry was so loaded up, she could hardly see him! She could just see the light on top of his cab.

"Aa-aa-choo!" sneezed Larry, and his light flashed. He was happy to be working with Joey, but his hayfever made him sneeze a lot. The top bales wobbled dangerously.

Roxy waved at them both and watched Joey zooming around. He certainly was the fastest digger in town!

Roxy had lots to do today, so she carried on working. She was moving animal feed to all the fields.

Doug and Freddie were working in the same field. Freddie was cutting the hedges and Doug was carrying sugar beet back to the barn.

Freddie was in a hurry. After cutting the hedges, he had to pull the plough and mow the grass.

"Hey, Doug!" he broomed. "I'll race you!"

Doug was in the mood for a race. He needed to move the sugar beet quickly, and it wasn't nearly as heavy as the rocks and sand he usually carried. A race would keep them both moving fast! He fired up his engines and got into gear.

"Ready, Freddie, GO!" Freddie laughed, and he and Doug rushed off down the field.

Doug bounced out of the gate and along the track, with sugar beets flying everywhere.

Joey had finished nearly all of his jobs. He'd been working extra fast to show how good he was at getting things done. He was covered in mud and grass, but he didn't mind.

Roxy looked over from her field. "Beep beep!" she tooted, as Freddie came into view.

"Sorry, Roxy! No time to chat! I'm mowing the grass next!"

"Erm, then why are you pulling the plough? And chewing up the track as you go?" asked Roxy.

Freddie slowed down and looked behind him. His plough blades were digging up the dirt.

"Oops!" said Freddie.

"Erm, wrong attachment. What a mess!"

Freddie unhooked his plough. He joined Joey, Larry and Roxy in the field. Roxy had delivered all her animal feed and was having some fun.

They had discovered that their tracks all had different patterns, and were doing a few dance moves to draw pictures on the ground.

Larry put down his load of straw, and showed off some of his best moves.

"Hey, Larry – nice lambada!" whistled Roxy, and Larry blushed. He reversed straight into his bales and knocked them over. Pieces of straw flew in the air.

"Aa-aa-TCHOOOOEE!" he sneezed, and scattered the straw everywhere.

Freddie took one look and decided to leave. He would find Doug and start mowing the grass.

Joey followed Freddie out of the field. They hurried down to the farmyard to look for Doug.

"Hey, Elvis! Where's Doug?" they asked.

"He headed that way – oops!" Elvis swung around with his long arm outstretched, and knocked over a large pile of wooden poles. He looked embarrassed. He decided to look for Doug as well.

Rex finished rolling and turned to talk to Elvis. He might not be as fast as the others, but he knew he always worked hard. He'd done a good job today.

Instead of seeing Elvis, all Rex saw was a mess. There were wooden poles scattered across the yard. He would have to ask someone to clear them up.

He trundled off to the fields, and wondered why the track was all ploughed up. There were sugar beets all over the place too.

"What's been happening here?" he wondered.

Rex drove past a field that had straw scattered everywhere. The soil was covered in tyre marks. The next field had a big pile of animal feed in the middle. In the field opposite, the hedge had been cut in a very wobbly line, with long, untidy bits sticking out.

"I thought we were spending today tidying up? The farm is in more of a mess than when we started!" Rex thought to himself.

Soon, Rex heard the others. They were being very loud, shouting and laughing. He turned the corner and found them.

"Ahem!" said Rex, over the noise.

They all went quiet and looked surprised. Rex didn't usually like everyone looking at him.

Rex blushed and spoke quietly. "I thought we were supposed to be tidying up today?"

The others shuffled their tracks and looked at their buckets in shame.

Rex wasn't the sort of vehicle to boss people around. He was better at asking nicely for things.

"Don't you think you should go back and sort out the mess?" he suggested.

One by one, the others fired up their engines and moved away. It was going to take them ages to make the farm look tidy. They knew they should have worked harder and done things properly the first time.

"Larry, don't go near any more straw," said Joey. "We don't want you sneezing again. Elvis, watch what you're doing with your long arm and double-speed digging."

Roxy led the way for Freddie and Doug. "Freddie, I think you should slow down and be more careful. And Doug, I'm surprised at you! No

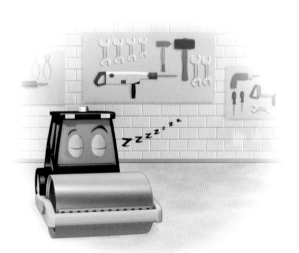

more racing, okay? And I guess I've got some animal feed to collect."

Rex settled into his corner of the shed for a small snooze. He couldn't help the others and had worked hard all day. And after all, they were actually tidying up after their own tidying up!

A CLEAN MACHINE

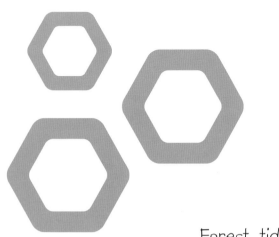

"Good morning, everyone!" smiled Sam, the foreman. He pulled open the large shed doors to let daylight flood in.

One by one, the JCBs opened their eyes. "Where are we going today?" Sam explained. Their job was in Bamford Forest, tidying up a clearing.

They all needed to work together to move fallen logs, clear the rubble, and flatten the ground. It was going to be a visitor park.

"Sounds tree-mendous!" joked Joey.

The others groaned. "Come on, let's get moving," said Sam.

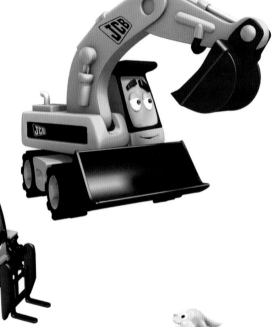

"It's time to roll!" smiled Rex, when they reached the forest. There was a large space with no trees. His job was to make it as flat as possible.

Elvis, Larry and Doug were moving away the biggest logs. "Come along, chaps!" shouted Doug. "Load me up!"

"Vroom! Vroom!" revved Joey. He and Roxy were digging at one side of the clearing. If they finished that, they could start work on building a forest lodge.

Joey revved again and spun his wheels in the dirt. "It's not very muddy," he complained.

"Don't worry about that, Joey," said Roxy. "Just keep digging!"

Larry couldn't stop sneezing.

"Aa-aa-choo!" he went, over and over again. "I dink I'b allergic to dis dust," he sniffed.

Poor Larry. Every time he moved, a cloud of dust and pine needles flew into the air.

Doug took him to the side. "I think you and Roxy should help each other," he said. "And get away from all this dry, dusty stuff. Roxy, take Larry to the main car park and load up with wood to build the lodge."

Larry and Roxy headed out of the forest. Behind them, a mist of flies, seeds and dry soil flew up into the air.

"Aa-aa-TCHOOOOEE!" sneezed Larry, making even more dust swirl around.

Joey was working hard, as always, but he wasn't in a very good mood. He missed Roxy, and he missed something else, too.

"I thought this job was going to be a nice, muddy one," he moaned. "I was looking forward to getting really dirty."

Elvis shouted across to Joey. "You're doing a good job, there, Joey!"

"Humph," replied Joey. He did a little dance to cheer himself up. He tried a cha-cha-cha but the pine needles made his wheels spin. He did a tango but the dust got in his engine and made him cough. He even did a few street dance moves but stones got stuck in his tyres.

Joey gave a big sigh and carried on digging.

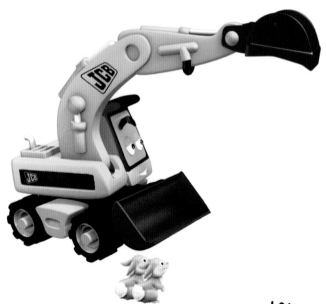

It was lunchtime and everyone was having a rest.

"Who wants to play hide and seek?" peeped Freddie. "I'll count, you all hide!"

Freddie closed his eyes and started to count.

Joey trundled off into the forest. "I'd rather play mud wrestling," he mumbled. "Or splat-a-cake. Or stick-in-the-mud."

"Coming, ready or not!" cried Freddie.

Joey looked around for somewhere good to hide. There was a big ditch to his left. He could try to hide in there. He changed into his lowest gear and moved slowly down the slope.

PLOP! Joey's face broke into a big smile. Mud – he'd found a hiding place with MUD in it! Hurray!

Squelch! Sluuuuuurp! Thhhhhhhhp! Joey nearly shouted out loud, he was so happy – but then Freddie would find him straight away, so he kept quiet.

Joey wriggled a bit deeper. He could hear Freddie rustling in the trees at the other side of the clearing.

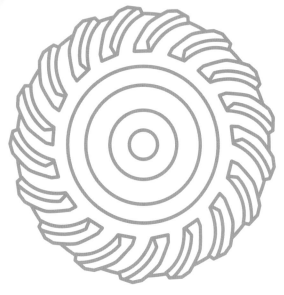

Freddie soon found Elvis, who was too big to hide properly. Rex wasn't really playing, just having a snooze in the trees, so he was easy to see.

Doug was next. Joey heard Freddie laugh and shout, "I see you, Doug! Out you come!"

Joey was so happy to be dirty again. He didn't care whether Freddie found him or not.

"Seen you, Joey!" cried Freddie, from the top of the ditch. "Out you come!"

Joey smiled and tried to climb out. "Erm – I can't," he gasped. "I'm stuck!"

Joey tried and tried to turn his wheels and drive back up the slope. Every time he revved his engine, his tyres sank deeper into the mud.

"Elvis! Rex! Doug! Help!" shouted Freddie and Joey.

The others drove over to see what was wrong.

"Ah!" said Elvis.

"Oh!" peeped Rex.

"Ahem!" sputtered Doug. "Well, let's see what we can do with you, you mucky pup!"

Doug threw a rope into the ditch and Joey held on tight. Doug revved and revved. Joey moved a tiny bit forwards, but was still stuck.

"Let me try," said Elvis, and took the rope. Slowly and steadily, he drove away from the ditch. As he moved, Joey moved too.

Eventually, Joey was totally out of the mud. "Phew, thanks Elvis!" he said. "I thought I was going to be stuck in there all day!"

Joey looked back at the ditch as if he quite liked the idea of being

stuck in the mud for longer. Then he shook himself and drove back with his friends.

"Well, well, well, what's happened here?" asked Cyril, the mechanic, when the JCBs drove back into the yard. "Joey, what HAVE you been up to?"

Cyril got out the hosepipe and washed Joey from top to tyre. Joey grinned and wriggled as the mud trickled down his windscreen. He was so happy that his dusty day had turned out like this.

Cyril made sure that Joey was sparkling clean. Then he stood back to check he hadn't missed any muddy patches.

"The thing I don't understand," he said, "is how you got like this on such a dry day. Everyone else is covered in dust. You must have been working extra hard."

"Oh, you know me, Cyril," grinned Joey. "I like to get stuck in!"

RACING AROUND

Sam had some very exciting news. Today was race day, and Larry was helping out at the racetrack.

The others were all going along to keep him company and see what it was like at a motor race.

"Will Max be there?" asked Larry. Larry was used to working at the racetrack, and he loved meeting up with his record-breaking friend.

"Yes, he'll be on show today," replied Sam.

Everyone was looking forward to seeing the race.

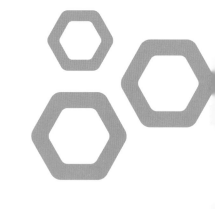

The JCB gang arrived at the racing ground. Larry led the way. They trundled past long queues of people, and right to the edge of the track.

Larry pointed to a large patch of small, grey stones.

"That's a gravel pit," he explained. "If a car crashes, the stones slow the car down straight away. That stops it from crashing into anything else."

"Wow!" said Freddie. "Do the cars go SO fast?"

"Faster than you can imagine!" said Larry. "And they're really noisy!"

"Hey, look, there's Max!" said Elvis. He waved and they all went over to say, "Hello".

Max was very pleased to see his friends. He was proud of his world record, and the racing ground was one of his favourite places.

"Are you racing here today?" asked Roxy.

"Oh, no, no, no. This track is too small for me. I need an even longer stretch of track to go at my top speed!" said Max.

"That's so cool!" breathed Joey. "What's it like to go so fast?"

"Well, I can hardly describe it," said Max. "Imagine doing your favourite dance, and spinning through the air like you have wings instead of wheels. That's kind of how great it feels."

Rex tried to imagine what it felt like to go so fast. He couldn't. He liked going slow.

Rex turned to Roxy to tell her, but he couldn't see her for all the people crowding around.

Max was still talking. He was telling them about the showroom he'd been living in, and all the people who had come to take photos of him.

There were lots of people taking photos at the racetrack, too. Doug gave them his best smile, but nobody took any notice.

Max explained that he had his own place to park in today. Special people had a ticket to come and see him. He'd heard that a King was coming from a far away land, especially to meet Max!

As Max drove off with a roar of his mighty engine, the others felt a bit lost.

"Let's go and look at the workshops," suggested Roxy. "We might see Larry again."

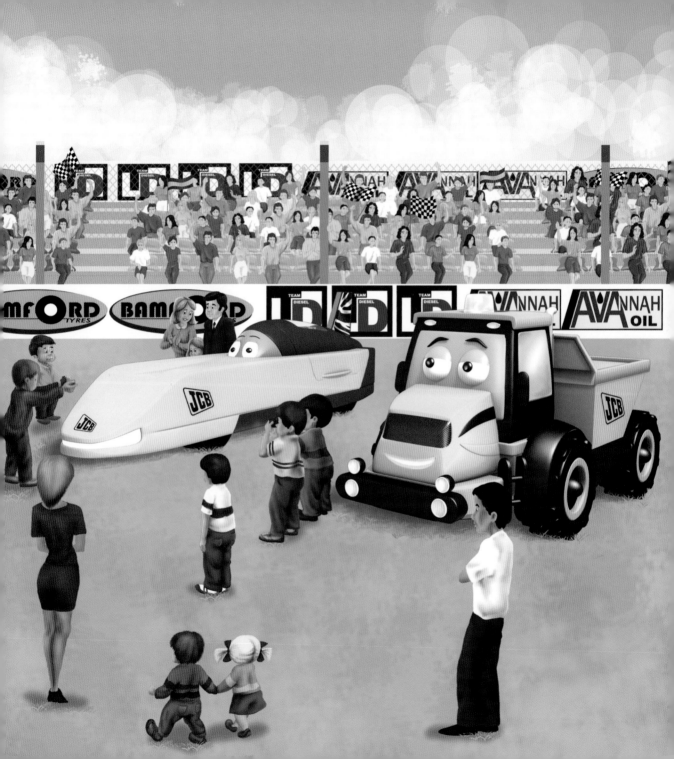

As they chugged their way through the crowds to the workshops, the noise got louder and louder.

"Can you *see* Larry?" asked Roxy.

"PARDON?" shouted Joey. "I can't hear you for all the engines."

Freddie was interested in all the machines and tools. Teams of mechanics in greasy overalls were rushing around. It was their job to check that the racing cars were safe and ready. Cyril would have loved it.

Roxy jumped as the racing car next to her revved its engine. It smelt of engine oil and exhaust fumes. She felt a little bit sick and reversed out of the way.

Larry was nowhere to be seen, and a mechanic told them off for being in the workshop. He waved his spanner and told Doug to get them out of the way. They all headed outside for some fresh air.

Doug led them towards a grandstand full of seats. People sat and cheered, and stood and shouted, and jumped up and down and screamed. It was giving Doug a headache.

"There's Larry!" revved Elvis, who was big enough to see above the crowds. Roxy couldn't see a thing. Usually, she would have asked Larry to lift her up, but he had much more important things to do today.

"Look up there!" beeped Joey. There was a traffic light hanging right over the track, with five red lights on it. One by one the lights lit up. The crowd were getting even noisier.

Then all five lights went out and the crowd went mad. Every car on the track revved its engine and set off at full speed. Roxy still couldn't see, but she could hear. The noise was deafening.

"I think I'm going to wait outside," she peeped to Joey, and drove off.

124

Joey and Freddie followed Roxy to the back of the grandstand. Rex, Doug and Elvis were close behind.

"I don't think I like racing day," mumbled Roxy.

"I thought I was ready for anything, but I wasn't ready for this," said Joey.

The others all agreed. Even Elvis, the biggest digger in the team, was having no fun. "I thought we were noisy and busy, but racing cars are a hundred times worse!" he said.

Rex suggested that it was a good time to go home. He led the way through the crowds and past the smelly workshops. They waved goodbye to Max, who was having his photo taken with a man in long robes and dark sunglasses.

They tooted at Larry, who was waiting at the edge of the track in case any cars span onto the gravel. "See you at home!" they shouted. "We're going for some peace and quiet!"

126

Cyril, the mechanic was in the shed when they arrived home.

"You lot look worn out!" he said. "I thought you had the day off!"

They all parked quietly and turned off their engines. Cyril brought some cups of nice warm engine oil to settle them.

They all agreed that racing was hard work – even just watching it. They had much more fun working together to get their jobs done.

"I'm totally worn out," sighed Elvis.

"Me too," sighed Joey. "Even my tyres are tired."

"More than that," puffed Freddie. "My exhaust is exhausted!"

Everyone chuckled quietly. Well, everyone except Rex, who was already fast asleep.

DIRTY DANCING

The JCB gang had been busy all day. They were driving back to the shed for the night.

"Whew!" whistled Freddie. "I'm so tired!"

"I just want to sleep," chugged Rex.

"Me too," said Larry, and gave a huge yawn. "But we need to get clean first."

"It's only mud," said Roxy. "It washes off!"

Cyril, the mechanic joined the gang in the shed. "Let's get rid of some of this dirt!"

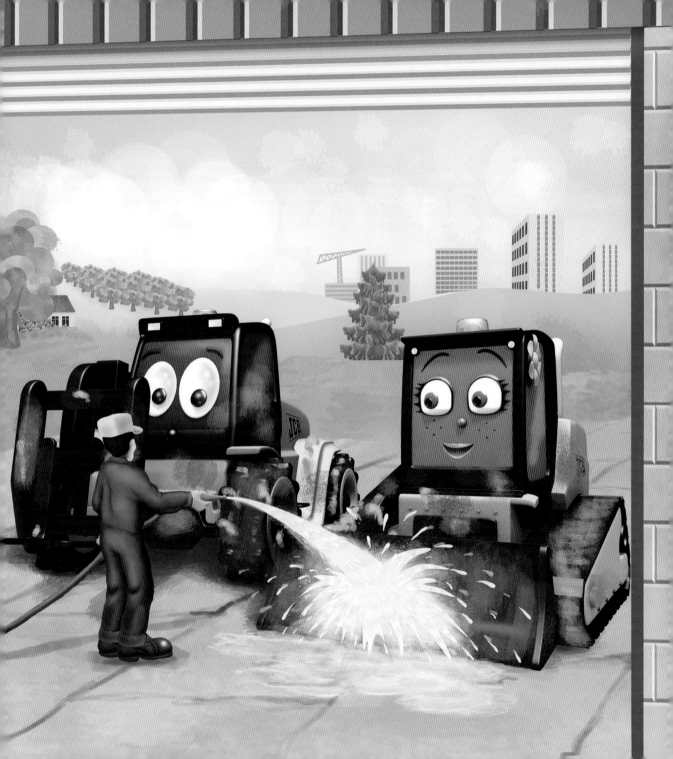

Cyril unwound the hosepipe. He got out a huge brush and a big sponge.

"Lovely – a nice, hot wash," said Doug. "With lots of bubbles!" He revved his engine happily.

Joey didn't really want to get cleaned up. He quietly reversed into a corner and hoped that Cyril wouldn't see him.

"Out you come, Joey!" smiled Cyril. "Look at the state of you! I'd better get out the pressure washer, I think!"

Joey scowled. He liked being dirty.

Cyril worked his way along the line of JCBs. One by one, he covered them in soap bubbles. They had soapsuds in their eyes, on their wheels, in their radiators and even down their exhausts.

"Aa-WHOOSH-oo!" sneezed Larry, as Cyril tickled his nose with the sponge. Bubbles flew everywhere.

Roxy giggled as Larry blew suds in her face. She revved her engine gently, and a stream of glistening bubbles floated out of her exhaust.

"Woah!" exclaimed Larry, "They're—"

"Shh!" said Roxy. "Look."

She pointed over to the shed doors. Sam, the foreman had arrived, and was talking to Cyril. They both looked very worried.

Cyril hurried off and Sam came to speak to the gang.

"Cyril has to sort out a problem at home," he explained. "So he can't finish washing you right now. He'll be back soon. I don't want you lot making ANY mess while he's gone, do you understand?"

"Yes, boss," they all tooted quietly. They liked Cyril and hoped that everything was going to be okay.

As Sam walked off, Joey drove
into the middle of the shed
floor. He shook his backhoe
hard to get rid of the bubbles.

"At least I can stay dirty for a bit
longer!" he smiled, and shook some more.
Bubbles sprayed everywhere.

"Hey!" shouted Freddie. "Good move,
Joey! Watch this!"

Freddie zoomed in a circle and then
braked hard. He skidded round and round.

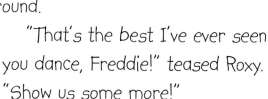

"That's the best I've ever seen
you dance, Freddie!" teased Roxy.
"Show us some more!"

Joey and Freddie did some
funky moves on the soapy floor.
They both laughed and sang
together.

"At the car wash – woo!
Talking about the car wash, yeah!"
It was brilliant fun.

Elvis picked up one of Cyril's hosepipes. He squirted it at Joey, who spluttered and coughed.

"My turn now!" said Elvis, and spun his big bucket around and around. He was still holding the hosepipe, and water sprayed everywhere.

Roxy joined in with Elvis's dance. "We should do 'Swan Lake'!" she laughed.

Elvis hooked his bucket under Roxy's tracks and helped her do a pirouette. "Just like Odette the swan!" he cried, twirling her in circles.

The others all cheered. "Nice one, you guys!"

"Ahem!" coughed Doug. Everyone stopped dancing and cheering. They thought Doug was going to tell them off.

"Don't I get a turn?" sputtered Doug, with a smile on his face.

"Yay!" cheered Roxy. She loved to watch Doug dance. He was actually very good.

Doug started with a few shuffles and slides. Soon he was dashing forwards and backwards with some very good dance steps.

"Psst!" whispered Freddie to Rex. "Pass me the pressure washer."

Freddie took aim with the pressure washer. He squirted it at Doug's body. Doug spun around in surprise.

"Woo-hoo! Nice twirl!" cheered the JCBs.

Doug looked a bit shocked, but then he smiled.

"Do it again, Freddie!" he laughed, and twirled around the room. Joey joined him, and they both waltzed through the jets of water.

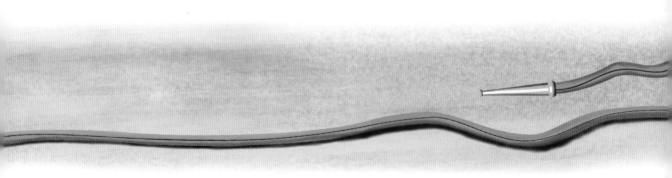

Roxy was laughing and cheering with the others, when suddenly she felt herself lifted off the ground.

Larry had hooked his forks underneath her and raised her high in the air.

"Hurray!" cheered the gang. They loved watching Larry and Roxy do lifts together.

They moved backwards and forwards through the soapsuds, laughing as Roxy wobbled slightly.

"Come on, fellas!" laughed Roxy. "Join in!"

Every single one of the gang moved into the middle to dance around Roxy and Larry. They had the time of their lives, swooshing through bubbles and splashing through puddles.

Eventually, Roxy asked Larry to put her down. They all realised how tired they were from their day's work.

Larry gently lowered Roxy to the ground. She looked at him and then at all the others.

"Oh!" she said, surprised.

"What's the matter, Roxy?" asked Joey.

"Well," she said. "I thought that we could call this our 'dirty dance' – but look at us!"

They all glanced around the shed at each other.

"We're not dirty any more. In fact, we're less muddy than when we started work this morning. What an excellent way to get clean!"

FEELING SMALL

"Good morning, everyone!" smiled Sam, as he opened the huge shed doors. "It's a foggy old day again," he added.

Joey and Rex peeped over Sam's shoulder to look outside. It had been foggy for days. Once again, all they could see was a thick grey mist swirling in the yard. They couldn't even see the other buildings or any of the trees outside.

"Ooh, yucky weather," said Joey.

"Yes – but you've all got the day off," said Sam. "So you can stay indoors if you like. Or you can pop across to see Max. He's been in the heated garage all week. I'm sure he'd love to see you all."

"Hurray!" cheered Larry. He worked with Max at the racetrack, and loved to see him as often as he could.

146

Doug led the way as the gang drove across to Max's garage. Max couldn't sleep in the shed with them. He was much too precious. He was the fastest diesel in the world, after all!

Freddie tapped on the window quietly. "Max? Are you awake yet?"

Roxy gently slid open the door and whispered. "Max? Wakey wakey! Good morning!"

Max slowly opened one eye. When he saw everyone in front of him, he smiled and opened both eyes.

"Hey you chaps, good to see you! How's things?"

"Oh, pretty good, pretty good," replied Doug. "What's your news?"

Max always had great stories to tell. The gang all settled in to hear his tales about world records, flying to other countries, and meeting famous people.

"... and then he said he wants to paint a special flag on my tail piece!" Max said proudly. He had been telling the gang about a famous artist who loved fast cars.

"Can we see? Show us!" peeped Joey excitedly.

"He hasn't done it yet," said Max. "It's the same old flag back there at the moment."

Rex couldn't remember what Max's flag looked like. They all reversed to make room for Max to drive out of the garage and show them.

"Vroom, vroooooom. VROOOOM!" Max fired up his mighty engines.

"Wait! STOP!" shouted Freddie and parked in front of Max so he couldn't move.

"Whatever is the matter?" asked Doug.

"Look!" said Freddie. "Right there!"

Freddie was right. In front of Max was a bird's nest with three blue eggs in it. If Max had driven even a tiny bit, he would have run over it.

Max gulped. "How am I going to get out? I can't stay here until the babies hatch! I have to be in America next week!"

Doug told everyone to reverse some more to make space for him to think.

"Larry, come over here. Can you get your forks into the space to move the nest?"

It didn't matter how much Larry manoeuvred, he couldn't quite get to the bird's nest. His forks were long and narrow, but his body stopped him from getting into the space next to Max.

"Let me try, Doug," suggested Elvis.

"Well, if Larry can't fit, I'm not sure how you're going to," sputtered Doug.

"But my arm is really long," pointed out Elvis. He reached out as far as he could.

Doug was right, though. Elvis was just too big to get into the garage and reach the nest.

"I can scoop it up and move it," suggested Joey. "I'm ready for anything!" Joey tried all of his best moves, but he couldn't rescue the nest either.

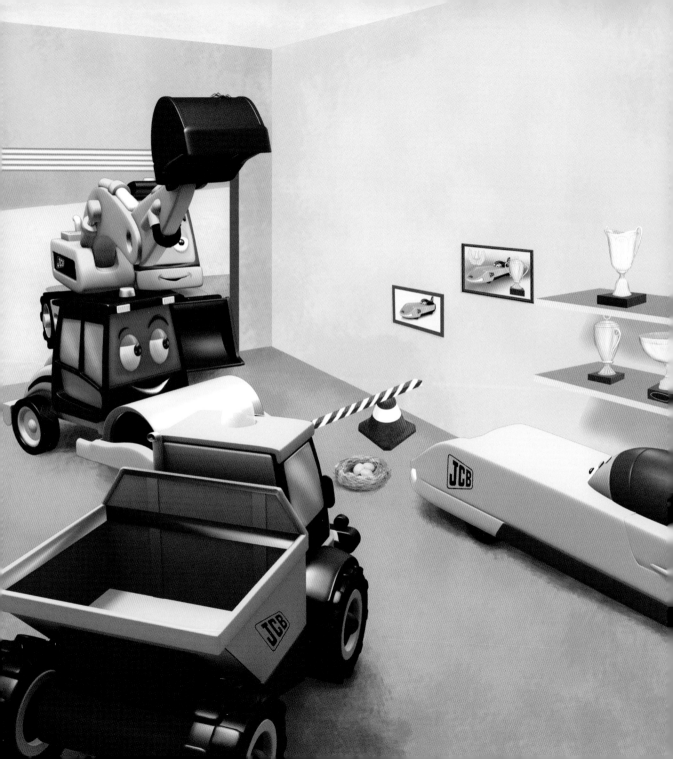

"I bet I can do it," said Roxy. She had been watching quietly while the others all tried and failed.

"Yay! Have a go, Roxy!" cheered Larry, and then blushed.

Roxy did a neat pirouette and moved gracefully towards Max. Then she braked hard and stopped.

"What's wrong, Roxy?" asked Doug. "You can easily fit into that small space."

Roxy didn't speak. She just kept staring at the nest. Then she slowly reversed and shook her bucket.

"I c-c-can't," she stammered. "There are sp-sp-spiders!"

"I say, old chum," said Max. "You're not scared of a teeny spider, are you? Well, I never!"

"What are we going to do?" asked Freddie. "Max can't move without you, Roxy."

Roxy gulped. She turned and looked at the boys. Joey and Freddie both smiled at her. "Go on, Roxy!"

Doug nodded. "You can do it, Roxy!"

Rex inched forward and gave Roxy a friendly nudge. "Don't be scared, Roxy. They're only small – even smaller than you!"

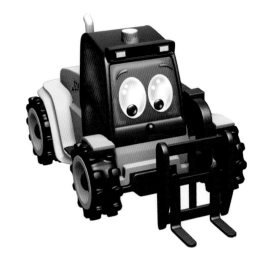

Roxy looked at Larry. He winked and blushed. "I'm right behind you if you need me," he promised.

Roxy did a neat three-point turn. She looked at Max, and then looked at the nest. She gulped three times and then edged slowly forward.

"Go on, Roxy! Well done!" they all whispered.

Roxy managed to slide her scoop underneath the nest. A spider ran off into the darkest corner of the garage.

"See, Roxy old gal – they're more frightened of you!" said Max.

Roxy gently scooped up the nest and lifted it ever so slightly off the ground. She reversed away from Max and looked for a new home for the birds.

"Here you go, Roxy." Larry pointed to a clean, dry shelf near the garage door. "Nice and safe – and no cobwebs at all!"

Roxy carefully pushed the nest onto the shelf.

"Hurray!" they all cheered. "Well done, Roxy! Were you frightened?"

"Hmm, yes," admitted Roxy. "Well – maybe only an incey wincey bit!"

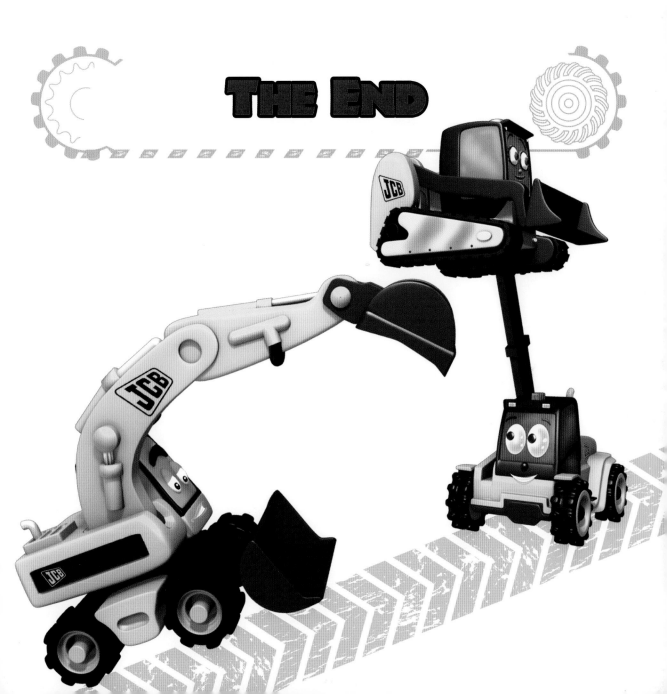

THE END

Bamford Business Park

Farmer Phil's Farm

BAMFORD

N
W   E
S

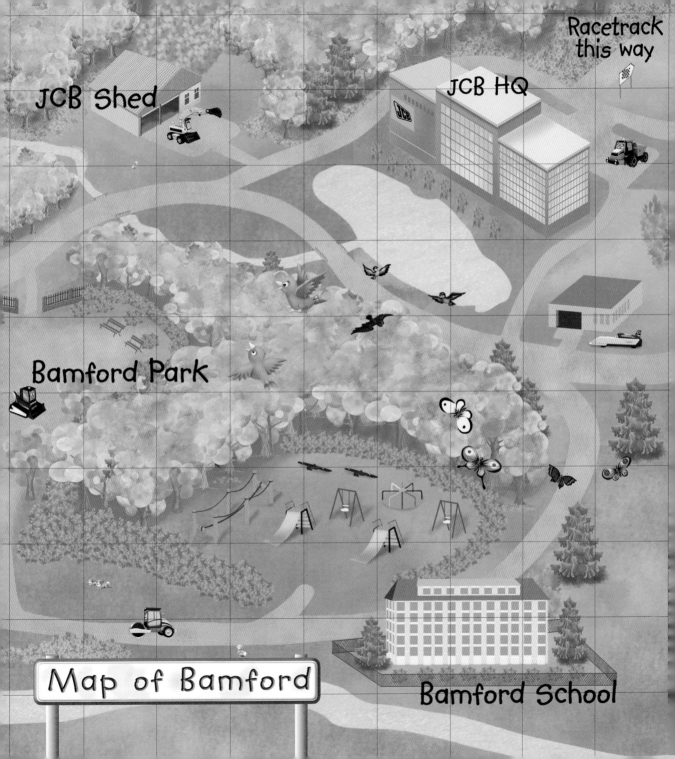

Racetrack
this way

JCB Shed

JCB HQ

Bamford Park

Map of Bamford

Bamford School

Written by: Lisa Regan
Illustrated by: Aleksander Panek,
Bartek Pawlik and Wojciech Kuzminski